God's mc
meadows,

TO
ST MARKS
UNITED
METHODIST

FIND JOY IN
THE JOURNEY!

DAWN
LAUCK
JER 29:11

Chariot Books™
David C. Cook Publishing Co.

WRITTEN BY ROBIN JONES GUNN

ILLUSTRATED BY DAWN LAUCK

God made everything.

Who made the world with its
deserts and shores?

"The Earth is the Lord's, and everything in it." Psalm 24:1

God did! He made mountains, meadows, and more.

God made the mountains.

Reaching to the sky where the winds
of heaven blow,

"He who forms the mountains, creates the wind." Amos 4:13

the mountaintops get cold, so God knits
them caps of snow.

God made the valleys.

With hills on either side, the valley
snuggles down.

"The soil in the valley is sweet." Job 21:33

Feeling safe and cozy here, the people
build a town.

God made the rivers.

When the snow melts off the mountains, it
makes the rivers flow.

"There is a river whose streams make glad the city of God."
Psalm 46:4

You can almost hear the water giggle as it
tickles the rivers' toes.

God made the streams.

Like busy little fingers stretching from
the river's hand,

"All streams flow into the sea, yet the sea is never full."
Ecclesiastes 1:7

the streams race to the ocean, spilling water
over the land.

God made the sea.

God filled the salty water with great whales
and fish galore.

"The sea is his, for he made it." Psalm 95:5

Then He told the foaming waves to run
and kiss the shore.

God made the deserts.

Tall cactus stand alone in the hot
sun all day.

"The desert will blossom with flowers." Isaiah 35:1, TLB

God sends a drink of rain and they sprout
a sweet bouquet.

God made the forests.

The forest is a home for birds, squirrels, and deer.

"Every animal of the forest is mine." Psalm 50:10

Aren't you glad God put them here?

God made the fields.

Farmers plant tiny seeds, then God
makes sweet raindrops fall.

"Open your eyes and look at the fields!
They are ripe for harvest." John 4:35

Out comes the sun to warm the field, and look!
The grain grows tall.

God made the meadows.

Where do the baby lambs go for food?
Do you know?

"The meadows are covered with flocks." Psalm 65:13

They frolic to the meadow where God makes
fresh clover grow.

God made the heavens.

Way up high, in the velvet night sky,

"By the word of the Lord were the heavens made."
Psalm 33:6

God watches over us with a million
twinkling eyes.

God made the heavens and the earth.

From the highest heavens to the deepest sea,

"You have made the heavens and the earth by your great power." Jeremiah 32:17

God made all these places for you and for me!

"The whole earth is full of his glory."
Isaiah 6:3